A LOVE TESTED

AMISH ROMANCE

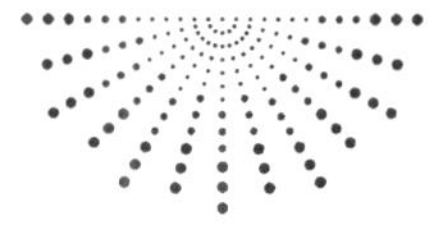

SARAH MILLER

SWEETBOOKHUB.COM

Abigail Freeman sat waiting for the arrival of the man she was about to marry. Birds were chirruping in the valley of Faith's Creek, frogs croaked in the Freeman's pond, the sun was bright and high, but in the heart of Abigail Freeman there was no love. There was only sadness and resignation.

Abigail was nineteen years old. Her blonde hair framed a delightful face with deep blue eyes as her primary feature. She was bright, but not overly so, decent and caring. Alongside helping her mother keep their family home, she also helped at the nursery herding young toddlers through a day of painting, storytelling, and prayers.

She didn't use to be sad in her heart. Once upon a time she had her whole future ahead of her with a young man that she loved. Jonah Harrison was her first and only love. They'd been at school together, though Jonah was a year older. They cut their initials into the family oak tree when they were new teenagers, and from that point, their marriage was a formality rather than a thing to be arranged. Jonah could make Abigail laugh by raising an eyebrow, which was all it took. And she could make him blush with the tiniest compliment. Everybody in Faith's Creek thought they were perfect for each other.

Which is why it was so sad that Abigail was waiting upstairs for the arrival of Samuel Marshall, a silver-haired accountant in his early forties, who was dining with the Freemans to discuss the final preparations for his marriage to their daughter.

Abigail nibbled at a spike in the corner of her thumbnail. She acquired the bad habit of biting her nails a few months ago. Her *daed* Wayne thought it was an unseemly act, but Maria, her *mamm*, knew that it came from anxiety and unhappiness so when they were alone she wouldn't chastise Abigail in the way that Wayne did. However, aware of her parent's displeasure, Abigail worked hard on not biting them in public; although when she was alone, like now, in her bedroom, she couldn't help herself.

It had been six months since Jonah was due to return from his Rumspringa, which meant it had been almost a year since she had seen him. She remembered with devastating recall the way he took her hands at the station and promised her he would make the most of his 'running around time' and return to her ready to marry, have children and devote themselves to *Gott*. They agreed the time apart would be so hard but necessary; that the absence would most certainly make their hearts grow all the fonder.

In his time away, Abigail kept herself busy by planning their future. She and her *mamm* viewed several small apartments since they wouldn't be able to afford a house for a few years. When they found the perfect one, close by her work and not too far from her family home, they discussed layout and simple decoration. Abigail also threw herself into her work and prayers, passing the time for when Jonah would come home to her. But he never did. Instead, he sent word via his sister, Beth Kemp, that he was extending his stay away. He could have sent a letter explaining his reasons; but all he said, via his sister, was that he wasn't ready to come back to Faith's Creek.

This wasn't unheard of in the community, and people went out of their way to reassure Abigail that young men like Jonah often need a little longer with their Rumspringas before they found their way back to *Gott* and to their intended. In fact, Bishop Beiler's own brother had taken almost two years as a young man before he returned to the fold. The Bishop and his wife Sarah were of particular comfort to Abigail in that first month and a half, as was her own *mamm*. They all said that Jonah wouldn't be able to resist coming back to such a sweet, caring, and loving young woman like her.

However, resist he did. After eight months of absence, Abigail wrote to Jonah asking for some kind of explanation. It broke her heart that she never heard back in person. Once again, Beth told her sadly that he wasn't yet ready. Evening meals at the Freeman's were becoming awkward. Wayne's patience was running out with his possibly soon-to-be son-in-law. He would bad mouth Jonah at the dinner table, and while Maria tried to shush him, there was a tone of agreement in her manner. Often Abigail would cry herself to sleep at night, wondering what she had done to be treated like this.

A month before the year was up, while the Freemans were at prayer in the King's barn, Wayne took his daughter to one side and suggested she put Jonah behind her. She was still young and would make a better man very happy. In truth Abigail had been thinking similar thoughts, she was tired of feeling permanently rejected. She wanted to feel loved. At work, surrounded by all the little darlings, she had been feeling very broody of late. Perhaps it was all tied up with Jonah not being there, but Abigail craved the love of a *boppli* of her own. She wanted to raise her own *kinner*, not just those of the community. So when Wayne pressed on that there was a decent man, Samuel, who worked at the bank that had inquired about her, Abigail consented to meet him.

Most people from Faith's Creek worked within the community, but not all could do so. Abigail worked at the *Englischer* nursery and Samuel worked at the *Englischer* bank, others worked in factories and retail, some at the local diners and restaurants. It helped both communities, the *Englisch* and the Amish. Her *daed* had told her that Samuel was particularly useful when someone needed a loan as he would help them navigate the paperwork. It seemed noble enough.

The first thing she noted was that he was so much older than her and that he dressed more smartly than Jonah ever would. He had about him an air of seriousness, but also the kind of confidence that comes with a life that had achieved a modicum of success. Together they walked along the river path. He pointed out trees and birds, demonstrating a vast knowledge of many things. He told Abigail that he would support her in all things, and that included her continuing to work if she wished it. He would love her dutifully if she permitted him to.

Abigail looked into his eyes and what she saw there was the opposite of Jonah. He wasn't youthful, impetuous, or unreliable; he was steady, caring, and predictable. She would have a good life with him, even if that life didn't include much laughter.

Later after she returned home, Abigail told her *daed*

that Samuel would do. That was all she could find to say. 'He would do.' And once again she cried herself to sleep.

So here she was, sitting in her bedroom, waiting to hear the sound of a buggy approaching. In that buggy was her intended, a serious and plain man, the exact opposite of the man she still loved. Samuel was coming to dinner. Abigail would sit by his side, hear his plans for the upcoming wedding, she would feign interest in his working day, she would serve him food she had helped prepare, and she would try not to feel like she was settling. Later she would pray to *Gott* for the strength to do right by a man who was offering her a future that Jonah had deprived her of.

In truth, Abigail was still shaken by the chance meeting that morning with Jonah's sister Beth at the market. It took her a few moments to recognize Beth. Having not seen her for a few months, the baby she was carrying in her belly had suddenly ballooned, and the way she walked and carried herself was so very different. Also, Beth was blooming, a radiance in her skin that made her glow. She wasn't a tall woman, and with her baby bump extending her outwards instead of up, she seemed even smaller than before. However, she also looked deeply happy and in love. Abigail bit down on her own jealousy and told herself it was unseemly to want what somebody else so clearly deserved. Her own time of being pregnant would come, and so what if it was with a man she respected rather than loved. She could still be happy — couldn't she?

When the two women's eyes met, there was an awkwardness between them. Jonah's prolonged absence had deprived them of being sisters-in-law, and the friendship that had been burgeoning had suddenly been cut down in its prime.

"Morning, Abigail," Beth said. "How lovely to see you."

"And you too," Abigail replied. "You look wonderful. Not too long now."

Beth patted her bump with a smile, saying it was a matter of weeks. Beth asked after her parents, and Abigail said they were well. Abigail then asked after Timothy, Beth's husband, who was well if busy. In the pause sat Jonah, whom neither spoke of. Until finally Abigail filled the silence.

"Did you hear I'm to be married?" she asked.

Beth blinked and held in a gasp, clearly she hadn't heard. "That is wonderful news." Though the way she said it, they both knew she didn't mean it.

"Samuel Marshall. He asked for my hand, and I thought... well... it's not like Jonah is coming back."

Abigail said it more sharply than she'd intended. After all, it wasn't Beth's fault. But there was a part of her that wanted Beth to send the bitter news to her brother with exactly that tone.

"Samuel is a good gentleman. He will treat you right." Again there was a tone of surprise in Beth's voice, and her choice of the word gentleman seemed to be a comment on his being so much older than Abigail.

"He is here. In Faith's Creek. That is a big plus in my book."

She didn't need to add that Jonah wasn't, and that was the point. Beth heard the unspoken intent. "My brother has acted terribly towards you," she said sadly. "I love him, but I can't defend his actions. In fact, I haven't heard from him in some time. All I have is a way to contact him when the baby is born.

Other than that, he's asked that I not contact him as he is tired of my remonstrations."

Abigail had a momentary pang of her own sadness at the knowledge that Beth and Jonah's relationship had been strained by this matter. But then she told herself it was all of Jonah's doing, not hers.

Surprisingly, Beth took both of Abigail's hands in hers. "You deserve to be happy. I wish it was with my brother, but he's let us all down. I hope Samuel gives you everything Jonah can't. And I hope one day you and I can resume our friendship. I miss you."

Abigail kept the tears in. She had done far too much crying lately, and she wasn't about to let Jonah's actions bring any more sorrow. But she too missed Beth and wished they could be friends. So she gave her would-have-been sister-in-law a squeeze of her hands in return, then wished her a happy birth before leaving the market ahead of the surge of emotions that were sure to come.

Those feelings were still racing around her head and heart as the sound of the buggy arriving could be heard from her bedroom window, quickly followed by Maria's soft voice at her door.

"Abigail. Samuel is here for you."

A self-protective armor fell across her heart. Numbing herself to the myriad of feelings, she stood, smoothed down her grey dress, adjusted her prayer *kapp,* and went to greet her fiancé.

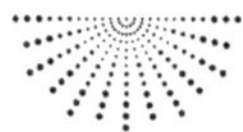

bigail Freeman served the potatoes to Samuel. He looked up at her, as she did so, with something that she thought seemed far from loving. It was as if he was appraising her, as a buyer might at a market. Finally, a smile broke out and he thanked her.

Abigail lowered her eyes and went to put some potatoes on her own plate. After the first couple fell, he whispered, "That's plenty." Shocked, she didn't put any more on her plate.

It was only as she took the dish of potatoes back to the kitchen that she realized she had complied with his wishes for how much food she ate without thinking. It had been an instinctive thing, and something she didn't like doing. As she took her seat next to him, while Wayne said grace, Abigail found herself wondering if Jonah would have done such a thing. She instantly chided her mind for going there. Jonah was in the past, the sooner she stopped thinking about him the better it would be for everybody. So instead she forced herself to change the question from Jonah to her *daed*. Had he ever instructed his *fraa*, her *mamm*, on how much food she should have on her plate? She couldn't recall a time, and if he had, Maria would have likely not served him anything else in protest. She might have even knocked him on the back of the head. Her *mamm* was no one's fool.

Immediately after grace, as they tucked into the delicious home-cooked food, Samuel was right down to business.

"I've got the use of the Brenneman's barn for the wedding. They owe me a favor or two, and have agreed to rustle up some food as well."

"I thought we were doing the food?" Maria looked uncertain.

"You'll be busy settling Abigail's nerves. It's a special

day for *Mamm* and *Dochder*. I wouldn't want to deprive you of that with menial duties."

"There is nothing menial about providing food for the day."

Abigail noticed then that Samuel's plate of food had barely been touched. He seemed to be pushing the food around with his fork rather than eating it. She felt sure, with the snub of using the Brennemans to cook, that he was unhappy with Maria's cooking. She felt insulted on her *mamm*'s behalf but didn't want to say anything in case she was mistaken. It could add insult to injury and make the whole thing worse.

Wayne was a natural peacemaker and acted as if there had been no slight, which made Abigail question her own thoughts again.

"That's a very thoughtful thing to do, Samuel. Do tell the Brennemans if they need anything, they only have to ask."

Samuel waved the comment away as if to say there was certainly no need for him to do such a thing. "As I said, they owe me. It's all decided. As are the hymns. A few family favorites that I've insisted be sung."

This time Wayne did look at Maria, and Abigail saw it. But whatever feelings her *daed* had were quickly swallowed down.

"However you wish it to be is fine with us. We're just happy that our Abigail is happy."

Her *daed* then looked at Abigail, a question in his eyes: *are you happy?* She was acutely aware that the past year she had been anything but happy. Her heartbreak had taken its toll on the family, her *mamm* had lost many night's sleep lying awake worrying about her *dochder*. Samuel was meant to be a way through the heartbreak, he was meant to be a road to a new future and a new happiness. She couldn't possibly say anything except, "Yes, *Daed*. I am so very lucky, and grateful to you for this union. And to Mr. Marshall for agreeing to it."

"Samuel, please," he said. Though the proud look on his face said he had liked the respect given by the use of the formality.

Maria, on the other hand, had been achingly aware that her *dochder* hadn't said she was happy; grateful, lucky, but not happy.

"*Gut*, then we're all agreed. What a productive night

this has been," Samuel said, pushing his plate of uneaten food forward a little. He then stood, to everybody's surprise.

"You're going?" Wayne also stood. Maria's face flushed a little at the sight of leftovers on Samuel's plate.

"I have work to do. Nothing happens by itself. If there's something that needs doing, make it so." Samuel then looked Abigail in her eyes, "This is my life mantra, you'd do well to live by it."

"*Jah,*" she said, but averted her eyes to the ground.

"I am sure I will see you before the wedding. I'll have my secretary check over my diary. Until then..." he leaned over and kissed Abigail on the cheek. She'd felt more warmth in the cheek kiss of a distant relative than the man she was about to marry.

There was an awkwardness in the room when Samuel's buggy had driven away. Wayne didn't know how to look at his *fraa* and *dochder*; instead, he looked out at the night sky and said, as if to convince himself more than anybody else, "I think this is a *gut* thing."

"Yes, I'm sure you're right." Maria had less certainty in her voice, but also wanted to think the best of the situation.

But Abigail wasn't so sure. It might be a *gut* enough thing, it might be something she settled for, and if that was the case she would make herself happy, perhaps even one day make herself love Samuel. The truth was, that since seeing Beth in the market, all bubbly, blooming, and so happy, Abigail had gone right back into that world of *What If...*

What if Jonah had a *gut* reason for not coming home when he did? What if he still loved her but now felt he had lost her because he'd not returned? What if she could actually talk to him? Face to face. Then at least she would know.

In fact, as she dropped Samuel's uneaten supper into the bin, Abigail became more and more certain that she just had to talk to Jonas. She couldn't possibly get married to this man until she had. She needed to know why he hadn't come home. She needed to know whether he still loved her, whether, in fact, he had ever loved her. Only when she had the answers to those questions would she be able to move on.

She'd tried writing, and that hadn't worked. She needed to see him face to face. Beth inadvertently had given her the opportunity for that to happen. Beth had also said she wished they could be friends again, and Abigail had a task for Beth that would prove whether she'd meant those words.

Abigail had a plan, and if it worked, she'd see Jonah once more. She would stand in front of him, look into his perfect eyes, and ask the questions that had been raging around in her head for the past year.

After all, what had Samuel said? *Nothing happens by itself. If there's something that needs doing, make it so.*

Abigail would live by her future husband's mantra, to find out why her previous suitor no longer wanted her.

CHAPTER THREE

Two days later, Abigail was on hot coals as she paced the floor of Beth Kemp's house. It was a modest home that had been prepared for the impending arrival of Beth's *boppli*. In many ways, it was the kind of home Abigail had been expecting to have moved into by now with Jonah. Instead, she was still living at home and planning a marriage to a much older and colder man.

Abigail's jangling nerves were infecting Beth, who now also seemed on edge.

"Sit down," Beth suggested.

Abigail did so out of politeness, but her jiggling left knee showed that despite being seated she was far from relaxed. Beth was also seated, her big belly protruding, her hands resting on its dome. Abigail looked at her and saw some of her own worries reflected back.

"I want to say *denke* again for doing this."

Beth nodded, but it was clear she was having second thoughts. "I did say I would help if I could."

"You've done more than I'd hoped."

"I don't like lying."

"*Nee*," Abigail agreed.

"Even though I understand why you asked me to."

"Don't think of it as lying. Think of it as a trial run."

Beth smiled, that was indeed a harmless way to think about what they'd done. If she could just make her mind believe it, she might feel a bit better about the plan.

Abigail had come to Beth the morning following the aborted meal with Samuel. She had implored her help in this matter. She was about to commit to a man that she was unsure about. One that was colder than the man she still loved. If she could just see

Jonah, if she could just hear from him the reasons why he hadn't come home, then she'd be able to move on.

In truth, Beth was also curious as to why Jonah had never returned, or why he hadn't even communicated his reasons, so when Abigail suggested a harmless white lie to get her brother back to Faith's Creek, she agreed to it willingly. So she had sent word to the number Jonah had given her, and now both she and Abigail were waiting on tenterhooks.

"What if he doesn't come...?" Abigail began but was cut short by the sound of an approaching buggy.

Beth quickly got to her feet and went to the window. She put a hand to her chest, a smile breaking out. "He's here."

Everything in Abigail wanted to leap up and see him, but she maintained her cool and remained seated. She could hear approaching footsteps that matched the wild beating of her heart. The door flung open, and Jonah burst through it. He was faced with his sister, standing there, clearly still with child.

"But...? The message said...?" he inquired, staring at her large bump.

Beth crossed to him, flung her arms around her brother, and kissed him on his cheek.

"I'm sorry, but it was a false alarm," she lied. "I sent word this morning, but you had obviously already set off. Still, it's so wonderful you're here."

Happy with the explanation, Jonah resigned himself to the fact he was here anyway and gave his sister a big hug in return.

"I've missed you," he admitted.

And Abigail had missed him too, she silently admitted to herself as she watched brother and sister embrace. He looked a little different, not just in his attire. He was wearing jeans and an open buttoned shirt with a pattern on it. But he was paler than he used to be, no doubt he'd been spending too much time indoors. He looked a bit more mature too, after all, it had been almost a year. Still though, thought Abigail, he looked as handsome as ever. If not, a little more, thanks to absence making her heart fonder.

As he pulled away from his sister's embrace, Abigail

saw him catch sight of her in the corner of the room. He literally took a step back, his face flushing red.

"Abigail..?"

She didn't stand yet, secretly afraid her legs might not hold her. "Hello, Jonah."

"What are you doing here?"

"I heard about Beth's false alarm, and called round to see if she needed anything."

A look of guilt passed between the two women, both aware they were playing parts in an orchestrated play of sorts.

Beth delivered her lines a little shakily, "Abigail has been great comfort lately. We are almost like the sisters we would have been."

Jonah looked down at his feet, nervously, aware of the elephant in the room. Finally, he admitted, "That gives me comfort too. Knowing that I wasn't here to support you, the thought that you two could remain friends."

Abigail now stood, feeling a little more certain in her composure. She didn't want to get straight into it, so she changed the subject slightly. "I hope you don't feel it a wasted journey. It really is lovely to see you."

Her words dripped like honey in his ears. She could see the stiffness in him drop away a little. She could see that he'd been expecting her to be angry, or confrontational, but here she was smiling at him. A smile that doubled when he returned his own, beaming across his face, crow's feet in the corner of his eyes, a twinkle in them too. Abigail so desperately wanted to cross to him, to take his hands in hers, to say how much she'd missed him.

But she did none of those things, instead, she moved towards the door, "I shall leave you both alone. I'm sure you have much to catch up on."

She could see the pang of disappointment on his face, and it made her secretly happy that she could affect him still. When she was at the door, Beth was ready with their agreed next step.

"Hey, I was thinking... Jonah, you're not going straight back, are you...?"

Taken off guard, he thought about the question. "Well, I was planning on staying a day or two to get to know my nephew or niece..."

"Good, then why don't I cook for us all tonight? Timothy will be so pleased to see you. And Abigail, you could join us... as a *denke* for taking care of me."

Abigail pretended this was the first she'd heard of such an idea, she blushed a little, "You don't need to thank me... that's what friends are for. Besides, I am sure Jonah would rather catch up with you alone."

Beth looked to Jonah, questioning if that were really the case. Abigail kept hold of the door handle, as well as the breath inside her lungs. She waited. Until finally Jonah answered.

"Not at all. It's been too long. I'd love it if you came to supper."

Just hearing those words, and the genuine glee with which he said them, melted her heart. Whatever subterfuge had brought him here, had clearly been worth it as Jonah wanted to see her. Beth could also see this, and it was clear to Abigail that Beth was also relieved that their cooked-up plan had worked. And no harm was done.

"Then it's settled. Supper at ours. Shall we say seven?"

Abigail beamed, "Seven is perfect. It will give me time to make a sponge cake. Raspberry and almond."

Jonah looked dizzy with nostalgia, which Abigail knew he would.

"My absolute favorite."

Abigail beamed, before she had worried her legs wouldn't carry her, she now worried she might float up to the ceiling, it was like she was walking on air.

"Until later," she said. Her eyes meeting his, holding them, keeping him in her gaze.

"I look forward to it," he replied. Meaning every word of it.

Abigail knew one thing then for certain. She didn't know why he hadn't come home, she didn't know why he hadn't replied to her letters, and she didn't know what was going on in his muddled brain.

But she did know he still had deep feelings for her, and that knowledge would carry her all the way home and back, to return tonight with a cake in her hands, and love in her heart.

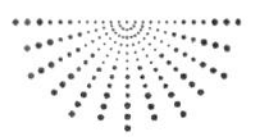

bigail took the cake out of the oven, and the smell that came with it was heavenly. She couldn't remember a cake coming out so well, it was the perfect shape and size, and when she pulled the testing needle out, it was as clean as when it went it. She heard the door open and close, signifying her *daed*'s return. Abigail felt giddy at the thought of him smelling the cake, she knew how much he loved her baking too. He'd so want a piece, and she'd have to tell him it's not for him. All her love had gone into this cake, she thought, as she placed it into a cake tin. She would serve it up to Jonah at the meal, and then she would ask the questions she had that needed answers.

"Mighty fine smell coming from this kitchen," Wayne said, coming in, and taking off his coat.

"Just something I rustled up," Abigail smiled. "But I'm afraid you can't have any. It's my contribution to a meal I'm heading out to."

"With Samuel?" he asked.

"*Nee...*" she hesitated, unsure whether to lie or not. "I'm going to Beth's house for dinner."

Wayne nodded, a deep thought crossing his brow. He hung his coat by the back door and washed his hands in the sink as he wondered how best to say what was clearly on his mind.

Abigail reached for her own coat as he did so, she wanted to be on her way. Being late was unthinkable right now.

"I saw the Bishop earlier, he wanted me to let you know that Jonah is back in town."

Her *daed* was drying his hands on a towel, but his eyes were fixed on her. There was no surprise in Abigail's hearing of the news, and she could see that her *daed* had already guessed she knew, and this was merely confirmation.

"Have you seen him?" Wayne asked, his tone serious.

"Beth had a false alarm. She thought the *boppli* was coming, but it wasn't. I called round to see how she was doing, and yes, it coincided with Jonah coming to meet the *boppli*. Apparently, word of the false alarm arrived after he'd already left."

When it was said like that, as a series of supposed facts, Abigail could feel the contrived nature of things. They sound false in her mouth, no matter how naturally she offered them. She could see that Wayne didn't fully believe her.

"And then Beth asked you to dinner?"

"*Jah.*"

"With her... and Jonah?"

Abigail swallowed, clearly he didn't like what he was hearing. "And Timothy too, obviously."

"But not Samuel?"

Abigail was taken aback at the idea of Samuel being there. It seemed almost laughable. "*Nee*, of course not. They don't even know him."

"Okay. But does he know?"

"I... well, he's busy... I'm sure he's much more important things..."

"Abigail. Sweetheart." The use of her name followed by his term of endearment meant he was close to chastising her. Rather than wait for it, she picked up the cake tin and prepared to leave. "You are engaged to be married. It isn't right that you're having dinner with an ex, and your fiancée knows nothing about it."

"I have no idea who Samuel is having dinner with. Right now he could be with all of his exes and I wouldn't mind."

Wayne crossed to her, not quickly, not barring her way, but enough of a gesture that she knew the conversation needed to be had. He looked down at the tin, "You've baked him a cake."

"Not just him."

"His favorite, if I recall." Abigail blushed a little at being found out. "It was something we had in common."

"*Daed...*" her voice was meek, she couldn't meet his eyes.

"Nothing *gut* can come of this." He rested his hand on hers, his fatherly hands, trying to protect her. "Jonah let you down and broke your heart. He had his chance, and he blew it. Samuel is a *gut* man, it would be wrong to treat him like this."

Abigail knew right then that her *daed* had seen through her. He wasn't judging her, rather he was looking at her with pity in his heart and it nearly crushed her. She decided to tell him the truth, it was her only saving grace. With *Gott*'s help, she hoped the truth would make him understand.

"I have to go, *Daed*. It's killing me, not knowing why he didn't come back. I've tried to move on. I am so close to being able to, but I just know, in my heart, if I don't hear from him the reason, then I'll always wonder. I'm doing this for Samuel, just as much as for me. I want to marry him with certainty, not with unanswered questions and endless what-ifs."

Wayne still held her hand. He'd listened to every word and didn't rush to answer her. With a faltering voice, he said, "I have a 'what if' for you. What if he doesn't tell you? You're going to have to find a way to move on eventually. Why give him the chance to hurt you more?"

Abigail lifted her chin, and proudly told him, "He can't hurt me any more than he already has."

"I wouldn't be so sure," Wayne said under his breath, but she heard him. She batted the idea away, not sure she could contemplate him being right. "What if I forbade you from going?"

This was her *daed's* last card, but it was a card they both knew he wouldn't actually play. It was a bluff card, and she replied by kissing him tenderly on his cheek.

"I'll be fine." Then she tried to part with a smile. "I'll bring you a slice back. I promise."

Wayne tried to smile, but it never reached his eyes, which had filled with water at their edges. Abigail didn't look back as she crossed to the door. Not out of spite or petulance, she didn't look back because she didn't want her *daed* to see the doubt that had seeped into her mind. Until now her plan had been based on Jonah telling her his reasons for not coming back or even contacting her. She hadn't even entertained the possibility that he might still withhold them. And she certainly hadn't considered that he had the power to hurt her more than he already had.

She walked the evening streets in a bit of a fog towards Beth's house. The evening was crisp and cloudless, stars twinkling in a clear night sky, but her mind was clouded, her heart was suddenly heavy. A gnawing feeling sat in the center of her belly. A creeping sense of pure dread. This could all go so very wrong. She had gone from the highs of baking a cake full of hope, ready to supper with the man she still loved, to realizing he obviously didn't love her because he only returned under the existence of a lie. He didn't even think enough of her to return her letters. And she was doing all of this behind the back of the man she was about to marry. As her feet took her to the gate of Beth's house, she was suddenly overcome with the urge to turn and run away, as fast as she could. Away from what might be the biggest mistake of her life.

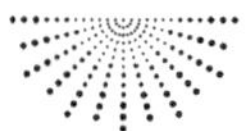

CHAPTER FIVE

Through the window by Beth's door, Abigail watched those inside. Beth, big and blooming, was laughing as she poured water into their tumblers. Timothy thanked her by pressing his hand on her big belly and leaning his head against it to hear his baby inside. His booming laugh could be heard as he felt the baby kick him in the cheek.

Jonah, sitting opposite, wondered what it was like to feel that, and Beth told him to go ahead and see. Abigail watched Jonah's face light up as his hand felt the tiny foot of his nephew or niece inside his sister's womb.

This window scene filled Abigail with an aching feeling. She wanted to be Beth, bursting with life, she wanted Jonah to be the father of her *boppli*, his hand on her rotund belly. She wasn't jealous of Beth, more than anything she wished her and Timothy well, but Abigail, who was once destined for the very scene playing out in her head, didn't understand where it all went wrong. She carried this ache, and confusion, with her as she entered Beth's house.

At her arrival, Jonah looked up. His hand still resting on his sister's tummy, and his big beaming smile was directed right at Abigail. So full of love for life, and for a second she saw the lust for life that attracted him to her in the first place. Caught up in the moment, Abigail thought that perhaps he too was wondering about their past and how they got here, because he got up, crossed to her, and took her hand without a pause for thought.

"I didn't say it earlier, but it really is *gut* to see you," Jonah told her, with genuine affection in his eyes.

"It's so *gut* to see you too," she replied and wanted this moment of connection to last forever. Though the conflicting doubts that had been sewn by her *daed* compelled her to add, "Maybe you won't be so keen this time to run off and never come back."

The mood between them crumbled, and a dark look descended upon him. It wasn't anger, but neither was it pleasant. He pulled his hand away and excused himself.

Timothy, unaware of the moment, saw Jonah leaving the room and playfully joshed him.

"There he goes, the master of quick getaways."

Beth elbowed him in the ribs, and catching sight of Abigail's sad expression, Timothy realized how callous that sounded.

"I didn't mean it like that. I'm just... it's so *gut* to have you back. That's all. We've missed you."

Jonah, from the door leading to the bathroom, told Timothy it was okay, he knew Timothy was only messing. Beth put a gentle hand on Abigail's back, supportively leading her to the table. As she took her seat, Timothy was still trying to dig himself out of the hole he'd just fallen in.

"I'm sorry, Abigail. That came out so cruelly. I just can't get over him being here. Turning up out of the blue like this. No reason, just here. And who knows for how long. It's confusing for everybody."

Beth gave Abigail a quick look, neither of them wanted Timothy to know about their white lie, he would be angry they'd used his unborn *boppli* in their subterfuge. Abigail imperceptibly nodded back, a sign that Beth needn't worry, she had no intention of telling him. However, Abigail was struck by how a small lie could snowball, she had recently lied to her *daed* about the matter, and now they were doing the same with Timothy.

"A brother doesn't need a reason to come home," Beth covered, pouring water into Abigail's tumbler.

"Maybe he needs a reason to stay," Timothy winked at Abigail playfully, once again not reading the room and Abigail's inner turmoil. She drank from her cup, happy to cover her face, so he wouldn't see how inadvertently cutting that remark was.

The meal passed happily. The food was delicious. Jonah quickly returned from the bathroom and brought with him a renewed humor. He regaled them with stories of his Rumspringa, stories of plays, music gigs, and comedy nights. With each tale, Abigail's world seemed tame, and a little bit colorless. Timothy recalled his own Rumspringa, which he'd enjoyed very much, but unlike Jonah, the shine had worn off quickly and he was very much ready to come home at the end of it. Abigail and Beth listened to both men attentively, passing smiles to each other from time to time. They loved hearing these lively stories, but the difference was Timothy's all ended with coming back to Beth, where Jonah's were all left hanging. Much like Abigail had been for the past year.

Her cake was wonderfully received. Timothy snuck an extra piece when nobody was looking. Beth didn't even sneak one, said she was eating for two and the baby was certainly loving it. Jonah's eyes closed at the first mouthful, he said the taste took him back to the first time Abigail had made one. It was a cake sale out of her back garden, he'd kept coming back to buy more, his *mamm* had thought he was greedy, but the truth was he kept coming back for Abigail. As soon as he said those words, the silence in the room was deafening. Everybody realized this was the one thing he hadn't done as an adult; come back for Abigail.

Finally, the night was drawing to a close. Abigail was sitting on the porch swing, taking in the night air and feeling like her dress was tighter than when she'd arrived. She probably eaten a bit too much, but that was because she wanted the evening to last and never end. She hadn't managed to ask Jonah the questions she'd wanted to. There had been moments, but when they presented themselves, she'd been enjoying his company too much. The white lie she and Beth had told to get him here would be for nothing because he would no doubt leave, and she'd declined the chance to ask him why he hadn't come back for her. She was feeling sad, and nostalgic, and confused, and a little bit let down by herself, and her lack of courage.

"You okay?"

Abigail hadn't heard Jonah come out. He signaled the seat, asking if he could sit by her. She moved up a little to make enough room for him. They sat together in silence for a few minutes. The sound of the night surrounding them. The crackle of the fire inside, a gentle wind caressing the branches of the oak tree, the running river nearby.

"Your stories make it sound like you had a wonderful Rumspringa," Abigail summoned up the courage to finally go there.

"It really was. I mean, I love Faith's Creek, but there's so much of the world out there to explore. I felt so alive. Everything was so new."

"I can see why you didn't want it to end."

He looked down, nodding. "I wanted that feeling to last forever. That newness. And it did, but not forever."

He turned his eyes to her, she saw a sadness in them that she hadn't noticed since his return. He continued, "But it faded, even the newness became old. I began to miss things that I thought had been holding me back. People." He swallowed hard, the final word coming out too quietly, "You."

Abigail exploded with excitement at the word. Her face lit up. He'd missed her. But that elation quickly turned to anger as she asked, "Then why didn't you come back?"

"Because I'd let you down. I knew you'd never take me back. I couldn't face the shame of living here knowing I'd lost you."

"But I wrote to you. I waited. And you said nothing. Just gave me silence."

He nodded, all of the same burgeoning in his face. "I'm worthless. I threw it all away on something shiny and new. I couldn't face what I'd done."

This self-pity infuriated Abigail, she got to her feet. A mixture of emotions raging inside of her. Love, anger, regret, and sadness. But right now anger was the most vocal of them. She bore down on him. "Even though you knew you'd be hurting me even more?"

He just nodded, tears coming to his eyes, he then lowered his chin.

She lifted it with her finger, looked him in the eyes. "I never stopped loving you. Don't you see what you've done?"

Those words were a spear through his heart. The joy of hearing them mixed with the pain of knowing how badly he'd let her down.

"Do you still...?" he stammered. Afraid of, and also praying for, the answer.

"Of course."

Both their hearts were racing now. All sounds of the night were silenced. There was no other person, animal, or thing that mattered more than these two. Right here, right now. The anger was still prominent within her, but it was being overpowered by her heart. She needed to summon up all of her courage to ask the one question remaining, the only one that she'd really wanted to ask, the rest was preamble. He stared into her eyes, willing her to ask it.

"Do you love me...?"

He didn't even hesitate. "*Jah.*"

She felt like she was underwater, like her ears were going to pop. The weight of his love was pressing down on her making it hard for her to breathe. She could feel his lips slowly approaching hers. There was nothing she wanted more than to feel the sweet press of his mouth on hers. To be kissed by him once more.

"Abigail! What are you doing?"

The deep voice shattered the moment, and the two stepped apart. It felt like her heart had been ripped out of her chest and it had fallen to the ground, shattering like glass, a million tiny shards at her feet.

She didn't turn around. Her face deep red. She couldn't bring herself to see the furious face of the man she was about to marry. Not in the presence of the man she loved.

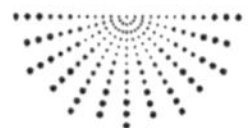

CHAPTER SIX

"Who is this...?" Jonah asked, staring past Abigail at the grey-haired man with fury in his dark brown eyes. Abigail was about to answer when Samuel cut across her.

"I assume you're the elusive Jonah Harrison. I knew your *daed*. Thomas. He was feckless too."

At the mention of his late father's name, Jonah bristled. Samuel put his hand firmly on Abigail's arm, and with a gentle pull indicated she should come with him.

"Take your hand off her," Jonah insisted, putting his own hand on Samuel's suit sleeve. Samuel looked first at the hand, then at the young man who dared to lay a hand on him.

His voice was ice-cold, "Let go, now!"

Jonah stood firm. "You let go of her, then I'll let go of you."

Abigail pulled her own arm free of Samuel's grip, then stepped through the linked hand and arm of Jonas and Samuel, thereby separating both of them.

"Stop it, both of you," Abigail said firmly, but quietly. She didn't want this to escalate. Turning to Samuel, she asked, "How did you know I was here?"

"I called by your house, your *daed* and *mamm* were having an argument about you being here. Like a little girl chasing after a teenage crush."

Jonah no longer bothered with the man, instead, he addressed Abigail, "Who is this ...."

Samuel stood tall, shoulders back chest out. "I am Samuel Marshall, engaged to Abigail, soon to be wed." This time rather than manhandle her, he put his arm around her shoulder as if gathering in his possessions in front of a hungry man.

Jonah took them both in, could this possibly be true? Abigail wouldn't meet his eyes, which he took to mean Samuel was telling the truth.

"You missed your chance, boy. Now why don't you get back to your childish Rumspringa, Nobody was missing you. In fact, nobody noticed you weren't here."

Abigail caught Jonah's eyes, of course, that wasn't true. She'd been missing him endlessly. He was confused though, she could see that, a minute ago she said she still loved him (and he loved her) and yet here was a man as old as their *daed* claiming they were to be married. Finally, Jonah had to ask, "Are you really marrying him?"

"What was I supposed to do? I'd heard nothing from you. I tried and tried."

"But look at him. He'll be dead before your *boppli* is even born."

Samuel balked at that, clearly, Jonah had hit a nerve. "I can offer her far more than your sharp tongue. Security, maturity, a good home."

"But what about love?" Jonah asked, but not to

Samuel, he was asking Abigail. No, he was begging her.

"I am not marrying for love," she admitted. "I tried love and look what happened."

She felt Samuel's hand on her once more, he'd had enough of this teenage nonsense. He had work in the morning, serious matters to attend to. "Let's go."

"I said," Jonah exclaimed, putting a hand on his shoulder, "Get off her."

Samuel pushed him backward, and he fell into the door, clattering as he did so. Jonah was young, but he was strong too. He quickly got up and was squaring up to Samuel, with Abigail near to tears between them. This was the chaos that Timothy came out to.

"What in *Gott*'s name is going on here?"

"Your brother-in-law came back to try and steal my fiancée, and if he thinks I'll stand for that...?"

"I didn't," Jonah shouted. "I only came back because I got word Beth was about to give birth."

As he said these words, Beth came out onto the porch. Her eyes locked in horror with Abigail.

Timothy was taken aback, wondering what on earth Jonah was talking about.

"*Nee* she isn't. We're weeks away yet."

"Well, that's not what I was told."

"Don't you think I'd know if my own *fraa* was about to give birth?" Timothy turned to look at Beth, his eyes asking her a question, waiting for an explanation.

Abigail couldn't bear it, this was all her fault. How had that beautiful moment just now on the porch, exclaiming their love for each other, turned into this? "I sent the message. To get Jonah back. It was a lie. I made it up."

The shock on Jonah's face was painful for her to witness. The disdain from Samuel she could ignore. But the downright disappointment that he'd been brought here by a lie, was too much for Jonah to take in.

Abigail defended herself, "What else was I supposed to do? You left me *nee* choice. And the worst thing is it worked. I got you here, and you were pleased to be here. With me."

"And now I'm pleased to learn how you've changed. Before I say anything I can't take back. You would never have lied like this before."

Beth wasn't going to let Abigail take all the blame, not for something she did out of love. "I was in on it. It wasn't all her. I wanted you to come back because I think she's about to make the biggest mistake of her life by marrying this man. And you, Jonah, you already made the biggest mistake by not returning from your Rumspringa. So yes, we lied. And we'd do it again. Because you're too stubborn to admit you were wrong."

The voice that came next was broken and croaked. "You lied about our *boppli*. The thing we both love the most. What if that lie jinxes us, and there really is an emergency?"

Beth turned to see hurt and pain on her husband's face. She hadn't factored in how hard he would take this.

Samuel was smiling at this sorry mess. "Come on, Abigail. Let's leave these people to their squabbles."

"Timothy...?" Beth implored.

But he turned his back on her, "Just go away. I can't..."

Beth, tears welling up, went back into the house.

This was all such a terrible, awful mess. Abigail saw what the white lie had done, the devastation that moment of deceit was wreaking. She had to salvage something from this tragedy, so she turned to Jonah, who was also struggling to hold his tears in.

"I was wrong to lie. I see that now. But I was desperate. And you're not blameless in this. We can make it all worth it. Let's go back to a moment ago. We were both about to settle our feelings for each other. And our future. We still can."

Her words hung in the air. She held both her hands together in prayer. Desperate for Jonah to do the right thing.

"My feelings for you have utterly changed. And we have no future. You are engaged to this man. He is your future now. And believe me, you both deserve each other. I am going back to the city. I hope I never see you again."

With those final words, Jonah walked away from her.

The thing her *daed* had warned her about had just happened. She had gotten her answer, and it was devastating. This morning she thought Jonah couldn't hurt her any more than he already had. But this night, in front of Samuel, under this full moon, he had shown Abigail that he loved her, and then smashed her love into tiny pieces.

Abigail broke down, more heartbroken than she had ever been before.

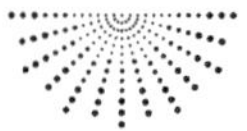

CHAPTER SEVEN

Abigail felt Samuel's patronizing eyes fall on her, as she struggled not to sob. Jonah was fading into the distance. Samuel took in a deep breath, and let out a sigh that lasted a long while. Finally, he came to her, towering above, and looking down on her both literally and emotionally.

"You're young, still. I will try to bear that in mind. I still believe our union will benefit us both. It's clear that your boyfriend wants nothing more to do with you. I'll admit there's a part of me that would like the same. But I am a man of honor. A grown-up. I will see you at the wedding. You and I will marry, and I will mature you into the woman that I, and your parents, believe you are capable of being."

That said he rested his hand on the top of her head and patted her. A gesture reminiscent of a teacher who has just taught a valuable lesson to a pupil. He buttoned up his jacket, nodded his head to Timothy, who was still shocked at all that had just happened.

"*Gut* night to you both." Samuel calmly walked in the opposite direction to Jonah. Back to his home, back to his work, back to his adult chaos-free life.

After wiping her eyes, Abigail blew her nose. She now felt Timothy's eyes fall on her and knew that the demonstrations weren't yet over. She looked up to meet him, and her expression said 'Go on then, have your turn'.

Timothy obliged. "I can't believe you used our unborn baby in your lies and plots."

Abigail nodded softly, he was right, it was an unconscionable thing to do. And yet, at the time, what choice did she have? She'd exhausted all options. She was trapped in a plan to marry a man she did not love, having received no word or contact from the man she did. Beth offered her help, and she took it. She did the only thing she could. Was it wrong? Most certainly. Would she do it again?

Probably. But she said none of this to Timothy. Because all the words had left her body. All the words she had wanted to say to Jonah, words of love, words of their future, words of happiness - they had shattered on the floor and lay in tiny pieces.

All she had left was a simple word of honesty, "Sorry."

She could see the word land on him, and while he may have wanted more, explanations, reasons, or even a bigger apology, he could see that she was so young, so heartbroken, and so lost. He took that word into his heart, and with the grace of *Gott*, he forgave her. She saw that forgiveness and it warmed her on such a cold night. So much had gone wrong, she had lost Jonah, was still engaged to Samuel, but at least this decent husband and father, and friend had forgiven her.

The tears were about to start again when an almighty scream came from within the house. Timothy and Abigail's eyes widened, staring at each other until Abigail said what they both knew. "The *boppli*."

Abigail raced to the house, kicking open the door, rushing into the room to find Beth on her knees, clutching her belly. Timothy quickly followed behind.

"Beth...? Are you okay?"

"It's coming!" Beth panted.

"But it's still too early," Timothy worried.

"Tell that to our child." Beth signaled the small pool of water next to her. "They've broken."

Abigail and Timothy knew what that meant, the *boppli* really was coming, early or not.

"I'll fetch the doctor," Timothy turned towards the door.

Beth's fingers clawed at his sleeve. "There's no time." She let out a howl as a contraction took control of her.

Abigail saw Timothy's panic, his eyes alive with fear, paralyzed by that scream. She knew she had to take over. Samuel might think she was young and immature, but right now, she needed to be in control. She had seen her *mamm* help friends and was even present at the nursery when a young woman went into labor while collecting her toddler. Abigail told herself she could do this. And she also knew this would be the best payback for dragging them both into her mess.

"Go get some linens and hot water. You and I will deliver your *boppli*."

Timothy looked at her, a rabbit in the headlights. She was so young. He wanted his *mamm*, or the doctor, or anybody…

"Now!" Abigail ordered, suddenly seeming older than her years. Timothy did as he was told, and went running to fetch the supplies.

While he was gone, Abigail helped Beth to her feet. "Let's get you to a bed." Beth nodded, breathing through her contractions, and like Timothy, doing whatever Abigail told her to.

As they slowly padded across the room, tiny steps, pausing occasionally when the pain took hold, Beth said to Abigail, "I wish Jonah were here."

"So do I," Abigail admitted, once more feeling that it was her fault that he wasn't. There was no time for self-pity. She flung the feeling aside.

"Knowing he is so close, but won't witness my *boppli* come into this world...."

"I can go look for him, there might be enough time."

"How would you even know where to look?"

Abigail smiled. "He's angry. He needs to pace around a bit. Whenever he got like that, he'd always go down to the creek. The water would calm him down."

"You're right. And it's only a few minutes from here."

"I can be there and back in no time."

Beth nodded, but the nod slowed, her face grimaced and another scream came. Echoing through the house and out into the world. Beth was crying now, she was scared and in pain, "Don't leave me."

Abigail squeezed her hand, helping her into the bed. "I won't. I'm going nowhere. Not until this *boppli* is here."

Her decision was made. It was sad that Jonah would miss this wonderful moment. She wanted him to be here. For Beth, but also for her, whenever he was by her side Abigail felt she could do anything. But if this past year had taught her one thing, it's that even though she loved Jonah, she didn't need him.

Timothy came in with fresh linen and a bowl of hot water that spilled over the edges as he walked. He put them down. Abigail dipped a hand towel in the water and wiped Beth's brow with it.

She smiled at her friend then, and at Timothy, and with confidence, she asked, "Are you both ready to meet your *boppli*?"

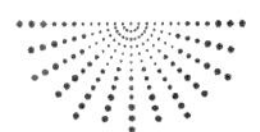

CHAPTER EIGHT

As Abigail had rightly guessed, Jonah was indeed down by the creek. He first came here as an eight-year-old following a fight with his *daed*. Jonah had been accused of stealing, which he hadn't, but had received the belt anyway. It all felt so unjust, and he left the house in a rage, but no sooner was he by the river, listening to the flowing water that even at such a young age he could tell that life and its events were flowing water. All things would pass. Since then, when a rage took hold or a sense of sadness, he would bring himself down to the creek, watch the river flow, and ask for *Gott's* guidance.

And he was doing just that now. Pacing by the river's

edge, underneath a twinkling star, occasionally looking to the heavens for help.

He had been so happy to see Abigail. She looked even more beautiful than he remembered. At first, during the meal, he had believed they could carry on despite his betrayal. Abigail seemed not to want answers, and instead took delight in hearing the stories of his Rumspringa. As he told her tale after tale, he began to wonder if they might just slip back into each other's groove, it was beginning to feel like he'd never been away.

But of course, he had, and of course, Abigail wanted to know why he hadn't come back.

The truth was, as he'd said, that he really was enjoying life away from Faith's Creek. He felt drunk on new experiences, felt their vibrancy, the fizz of continually doing new things. Faith's Creek was a wonderful place to live, but there was little here that surprised him. Even on his return just that morning he could see that nothing much had changed in his absence. So when the end of his Rumspringa neared, he became very anxious, a fear that all this excitement would no longer be available to him, so he'd decided to stay longer. To keep doing new things.

For a while, he felt certain he'd made the right decision. Of course he missed Abigail, but he tried not to think about her. When his mind strayed to her, he was overcome with deep shame that he hadn't even tried to explain why he hadn't come home. Her letters arrived, and he put them in a drawer, telling himself he'd reply one day; a day that never came. So the shame went even deeper. He knew he must be hurting her, but it seemed easier not to think about it and just keep on doing new and exciting things.

Jonah had become a master at burying his head in the sand.

He also buried his head about the fact that these new and exciting things were becoming less fun. The thrill he'd had at doing them was dulling against the things he was missing. His sister, the creek, the familiar faces, *Gott*'s love, and most of all: Abigail.

About a month ago, he had realized what an awful mistake he'd made. He was living in a city where all the friends he had were transient, where all the experiences he was having were shallow, and knowing that the one person he'd truly loved no doubt hated him. There was no way he could come back, he told himself. People would laugh at him, or they'd scold him for being so selfish. He'd even stopped praying for fear of what *Gott* thought of him.

But then word came that Beth was in labor, this was the perfect excuse to return to Faith's Creek. He was desperate to meet his new family, and even more so to see his sister, and to seek her advice on how best to come home. So it was with a joyful heart that he rushed into her house, and he couldn't believe how perfect it was that Abigail was there too. It seemed like it was a sign from *Gott*, that in wanting to come home he was making the right choice. This was backed up by Abigail's words of love. So when he told her that he still loved her, everything seemed to be aligning.

However, it was all predicated on a lie. Abigail had manipulated him back to Faith's Creek. Not only that, his sister was in on it. The one person he felt he could trust, the person he had come to for advice, he could no longer count on her impartiality. There were more lies too, Abigail was actually engaged to be married. And to such a pompous old fool. Clearly, all of this was a plot to get her out of a loveless marriage. If Abigail was capable of such lies, how could he possibly believe her declaration of love? She could have said it just to win him back so as not to marry that oaf.

Jonah's head was spinning, he didn't know what was up or down, black or white, who to trust. He thrust both hands together, fell to his knees, and for the first time in months prayed for guidance.

"Jonah...? Is that you?"

Jonah's head flipped around to see Bishop Beiler out walking a dog. The chocolate Labrador ran to him and licked his face. Jonah delighted in the dog's pleasure at seeing him and gave him a big fuss until he finally got back to his feet.

"Amos, it's so good to see you."

"And you too, my son." Amos pumped Jonah's hand in a familiar and welcoming shake. "I hope I didn't spoil your prayers."

"Not at all, in fact, I think you're the answer to them."

Amos cocked an eyebrow, unsure what he meant by that, but he had seen what turmoil the boy had been in when he came through the clearing with the dog. "Okay, so how can I help?"

"I need your advice," Jonah admitted, and the whole story came tumbling out. From the moment he left for his Rumspringa, right up to ten minutes ago when he discovered the lie that had brought him back.

Amos sat silently through it out, occasionally throwing a stick into the water for the dog to retrieve. "This is old man Byler's dog. He doesn't get walked much so I brought him with me. See how he doesn't think, he just enjoys what life throws his way?"

Jonah nodded, watching the dog splashing joyously brought smiles to both men. Amos sat down. Jonah gave him the space to think.

After a few seconds, Amos patted both knees with his hands and said, "Do you love her?"

"I thought I did."

"We all make mistakes; for some, it is staying on a Rumspringa without sending reasons why. For others, it is enlisting friends to lie to get them back. Mistakes can be forgiven. And if she loves you enough to forgive yours, do you love her enough to forgive hers?"

Jonah thought about this for a few seconds more. His estimation for Abigail had gone down by the lie, but given the way he'd treated her, he could understand her being driven to doing it. So yes, he could forgive her. So why was he still sitting here? Jonah then realized that the first lie was no longer the main issue.

"How do I know all of this wasn't just to get her out of marrying somebody she doesn't love?"

Amos nodded. "I suppose there's only one way of knowing for sure." Jonah knew the answer, but the Bishop said it anyway. "You need to ask her."

Amos was right. If Jonah was going to leave Faith's Creek again, or if he was going to stay - it all hinged on the answer to this question. Was Abigail merely looking for an escape route, or did she see her future with him and nobody else?

Amos got to his feet. "No point dawdling. Let's go and ask her." With the dog to heel, he walked the path back to Beth's house. Jonah took a few seconds, then swallowed his nerves, got up, and followed.

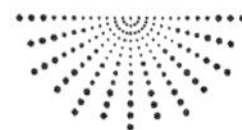

CHAPTER NINE

Abigail's ears rang as Beth let out an almighty scream. She could see that Timothy was scared by the sound. The man froze, his face white, his hands shaking but Abigail kept her calm, wiping Beth's brow, and assuring her that she was doing well. She could see the baby's head, it wouldn't be long now.

Abigail patted Timothy's shoulder as she moved around the room. Encouraging the man to move. Swallowing he took his *fraa's* hand. "Can I do anything?" he asked in a shaky voice.

"*Nee*, just shut up unless you want to swap places," Beth rasped between her screams.

Abigail gave him a small smile to reassure him that this was normal. The births she'd attended with her *mamm* had included some choice words and even louder screams. But she never managed to finish that sentence as yet another scream came from such a petite woman that they would've thought her incapable of such a noise.

The door burst open, and in came Jonah, panic on his face.

"I heard screaming. What's wrong?"

Which is when he saw his sister on the bed. For a second he looked like he might faint. Luckily Amos, who followed him in, had more experience in these matters. He shielded Jonah from view and looked kindly upon Abigail.

"Are you okay?" Amos asked her. "Do you know what you're doing?"

"I think so. There was no time for anything else."

"I have faith in you. You can do it," Amos said as he steered Jonah from the room.

"Is she going to be okay?" Jonah asked the panic raising his voice. "Why is she screaming so much?"

"BECAUSE IT HURTS!" Beth bellowed at him, and his eyes widened in fear.

"Let's get you two out of here, give Abigail and Beth the space they need," Amos gently suggested.

"I'm going nowhere." Timothy shook his head but he looked white as a sheet and Abigail feared he may faint. "She needs me."

"Abigail's got this. Fussing around will help nobody," Amos said in that way that was calm, quiet, and yet demanding.

As they argued, Abigail put them out of her head. She focused totally on Beth. Having watched her *mamm* she was aware of the decreasing gap between contractions and felt sure that Beth was nearly at the point of delivery. She leaned in, her mouth close to Beth's ear.

"Your *boppli* wants to come out. Let's do one last big push."

Beth looked back at her with petrified eyes, but Abigail met them with calm and clarity.

"You can do it. I promise you. It's all going to be fine."

Beth welcomed those words like the salve on a painful cut. She breathed in deeply, took hold of Timothy's hand, and pushed as hard as she could. A scream louder than any trapped bear echoed around the room.

Abigail spurred her on, "Keep going, you're nearly there."

Finally, the *boppli* was born. Abigail was holding the tiny bundle in her hands. Carefully, she cut the cord with the sharpest scissors they had.

Timothy kissed his *fraa's* cheek, telling her she'd done well. Beth was crying now, tears of relief and joy. A mixture of emotions raging around her body. As Abigail wrapped the boppli in a towel, Jonah looked over her shoulder in wonder.

"It's a girl," Jonah told the room. "I'm an uncle to a beautiful niece."

"A *boppli* girl," Beth repeated, as more and more tears came.

"Praise *Gott*, she's beautiful," Amos exclaimed.

Abigail was wiping the *boppli's* face as fear slid an icy hand down her back. The *boppli* should have cried by now, instead, she was so still. Abigail couldn't be sure she was breathing but tried not to panic.

The fact she wasn't celebrating was noticed by Jonah. "Is everything okay?"

"I... I... I'm not sure."

The room went quiet. The silence of the *boppli* was all they could hear now. Beth sat up, despite the pain, her eyes imploring Abigail to tell her what was going on. Timothy too stared at her.

Abigail froze for a second. She felt that the lie she'd made Beth tell and the stress of the arguments earlier might have caused Beth to deliver too soon. Or maybe she'd done something wrong in the birthing. Abigail was paralyzed with the certainty that this was all her fault. She looked around the room, at Timothy who was close to tears, Beth who was so frightened, Amos Beiler who was trying to give her a look of reassurance but underneath was a dreaded uncertainty, and finally Jonah, who looked at her with pleading eyes to just do something. To make this all right.

Abigail tried to remember what her *mamm* had done

after a *boppli* was born. And then it came to her. She put the tiny girl over her shoulder and patted her back with a little force.

Nothing. All those eyes. Even more scared now.

Once more, she patted a little harder.

And then the *boppli* spluttered. Quickly followed by an intake of breath, and then a welcome cry. She was alive. Everybody in the room could hear her. Beth held out her arms, she wanted her *dochder*. With a feeling of such relief that she was almost dizzy, Abigail gladly handed the *boppli* over.

As Beth took her beautiful *dochder* from her dear friend's nursing hands, she said "*Denke.*"

Now it was Abigail's turn to cry. Whatever mess she had caused tonight, in her heart she would always know, she had made up for it with this moment. Timothy touched her arm, and he thanked her too.

The *boppli* was crying now, and Beth was trying to give her comfort and her first feed. The men were fussing around, asking what she needed, providing new bedding, taking the old away.

Abigail, rightly, was forgotten. She had done her

work. She wasn't needed. And she felt a little like she was intruding on a new family's moment. So she picked up her coat and walked to the door. She took one look back and saw Jonah cooing over the *boppli*, Timothy beaming smiles at Amos, talking about being daeds. And Beth, who was in heaven, skin to skin with her bundle of love.

Abigail smiled and left them to it. Taking the stairs she left the house and began her walk back home. Back to her future with Samuel. A little sad, yes, but a little happy too. She had made amends, and would now accept whatever life was going to throw her way. She'd accept *Gott*'s will, and stop being a petulant little girl. It was time to grow up, and face the future.

"Abigail...?"

Her heart stopped beating, her lungs stopped taking in the air, her feet wouldn't carry her another single step. She didn't dare to hope, was this what *Gott* had planned for her? She didn't dare believe it because she didn't think she could take her heartbreaking again.

"Don't go," Jonah said.

Abigail froze, what now, was there hope?

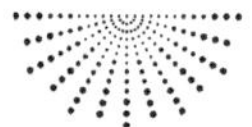

CHAPTER TEN

Abigail froze, her back to him. Still afraid to breathe, her heart pounded against her chest. She didn't want to turn around, because she didn't want him to see how much she loved him, to see how much she would hurt if he wasn't asking her to stay... forever. She heard his soft steps as he came closer, she felt the palm of his hand on her back. The fizz of electricity of what could be a platonic and chaste-friendly touch.

"Abigail, turn around." His voice was barely a whisper, but she did as he asked.

In his face she saw the young boy she'd fell in love with all those years ago. Also in his face, she saw the young man he now was, with new experiences in the lines around his eyes and mouth. He wasn't that boy, but neither was he a stranger. He had changed, but he was still very much recognizable. She felt sure, if they allowed themselves, they could slot back together like missing jigsaw pieces.

"*Denke*, for what you did in there, you were so brave."

She shook her head. "After the lie... the argument... maybe I'm the reason the *boppli* came early. It could have been so much worse."

"And yet by *Gott*'s grace, it is so much better. I feel touched by new life, by new hope. And not just by seeing my niece being born, but by seeing you right there in the heart of my family."

Abigail swallowed, she wanted to speak but the words wouldn't come past the lump in her throat, there were tears at the corner of his eyes.

"I have wanted to come home for a while now, but I've been too ashamed. That I wouldn't be welcome back." His voice faltered here, "That you would have moved on and would have met somebody else."

She looked down at the floor.

"Which you have."

How she wanted to tell him she hadn't but words wouldn't come. They stuck in her throat and she saw his face crumple. She had to talk and she willed her mouth to move. "I have an arrangement, but I haven't moved on."

"Is that why you tricked me back? To get you out of that arrangement?"

Now her eyes met his, how could he think such a thing? "*Nee*. Absolutely not. I did the only thing I could to get you here because I still love you. It's not Samuel I'm trying to escape from. My father arranged that marriage to try and help me escape my love for you. It wouldn't have mattered who he picked, nobody is you. I would've been trapped with anybody else."

She could see that her words were reaching him, a weight lifting off his shoulders and he looked taller. The cogs in his brain were turning and his mouth opened and closed before he finally got the words out. "How did we get to this?"

Abigail saw no point in lying, if they were going to get through this it had to be with the truth.

"You chose to continue your Rumspringa instead of returning to me."

His eyes shot up, was this accusation, was this going to be an argument?

Abigail shook her head to let him know she hadn't finished. "That was difficult, but if we'd talked about it, I could have reconciled myself to giving you more time. But your shame at your decision kept you from even talking to me, or writing to me, which only hurt me more. Your silence has left me in pieces. I have told you I love you. I have shown it, I acted so totally out of character to get you back here, I have angered and upset people. All so that we could talk... so that I could tell you. I have to know, Jonah... how do you feel? What do you want?"

She was right. It was down to him now. Everything she'd done, she'd done to get him here. He had to put aside his anger at the lies, put aside his anger towards Samuel a man who didn't deserve Abigail. Even put aside this swirling new love for his niece. He had to dig deep, ask himself what he really wanted. And he had to bite back his pride and say it out loud. If he didn't find the courage to speak now, his silence would trap him, and Abigail in a loveless marriage.

Jonah would be trapped in an unforgiving silence. So he dug deep and found the words.

"I love you, Abigail."

Her heart set off like a firework inside of her. She tried to contain its swirls and sparkles, those words weren't enough. She kept the explosion within and waited for him to continue.

"I want you to forgive me for how I treated you. I totally forgive you for what you've done to get me here. I can see you only did it in response to me letting you down. I want you to end your engagement with Samuel. I want us to try and pick up where we left off, to begin again anew. We're not the people we were, but we are still two people in love. I want a house like Beth and Timothy, I want a *boppli*, maybe two or three. I want to grow old with you and raise them under *Gott*'s guidance here in Faith's Creek."

She was weeping now and she let the love and joy she felt show on her face. Yet still, he continued. He took her hands in his.

"I want to come home. To you."

He moved his lips to her, and they kissed. There was a part of the kiss that, to Abigail, felt like sitting by the fire and reading the Bible. It felt familiar, it felt like old times. It felt right. But there was much more in that kiss. There was a newness to it. Like a new adventure, a vibrant experience, a hint at the future, and a fizz of right now. It felt wonderful. It was perfect. It was what she had been waiting for.

When the kiss was finished, and they stood under the bright moon, beneath twinkling stars, with the sound of the creek in the background, Jonah spoke. "What if the elders don't let me come back?"

She knew what he was asking. It was the final admission of doubt in their future, the last possible impediment. If he wasn't allowed back into the community, would she leave to be with him? Or would the mistake he'd made, if compounded by the elder's decision, be the thing that kept them apart? Did she love him enough to be with him anywhere? It was a big question, and once she hadn't thought about. It scared her right down to her boots, but then not being with him scared her more. She wasn't sure she could answer it, but she also knew that she had to, or they ran the risk of being once again in limbo.

"Let's pray on it," Abigail suggested.

A new shame came into his face, "I haven't done much praying lately."

Her face was gentle and caring. "It's like riding a bike. You just have to get back on. *Gott* is always there, waiting for you to come back to him."

She knelt down, feeling the earth beneath her knees. She clasped her hands together in prayer, and let her thoughts rise to the heavens. She felt him kneel beside her and knew that he would be doing the same. She sent up her prayers, asking for *Gott*'s help and guidance. They prayed in silence for almost five whole minutes. Until finally a deep feeling of peace and understanding flooded through her. She opened her eyes and saw Jonah, deep in prayer, eyes still closed. She pressed her hand against his cheek.

"It's going to be okay."

He opened his eyes, and she could see he too was flooded with the same feeling. Her words, their conviction, their promise, had brought peace to him, along with *Gott*'s love.

"I love you enough to leave this place, a place that is

my home my parents whom I love just as much but in a different way. I will tell the elders this, and they will see that our love is so big that I would give everything up for it. They won't want to deprive Faith's Creek of such a wonderful thing. They will want it here, to warm everybody in its glow. To see it as a guiding light."

His face flushed with the truth, and he knew she was right. He was overcome with such a sense of rightness, of coming home, of being right where he belonged, next to the woman he belonged with.

They would convince the elders. And with *Gott*'s help, they would make their home, their family, their future. It suddenly seemed so very simple, and he was ashamed of how he had almost thrown it all away. Abigail could see that, could also see a glimpse of the unhappy future that had been planned with Samuel.

She shook her head, and with it, she shook out all negative feelings.

"None of that matters now," Abigail told him. "Only the here and now, and the soon to be."

As she stood, with a lightness in her heart she hadn't

felt for some time, he remained on his knees. Or, more precisely, he went to one knee. His hand took hers, and he beamed up at her. She wanted to giggle, she wanted to cry. She wanted to sing.

"Will you marry me, Abigail Freeman?"

She couldn't help it, a little giggle of pure glee escaped her lips.

"Try stopping me."

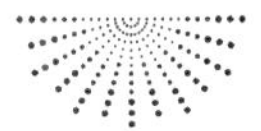

Six months later Abigail was crying like the world was about to end. Her eyes streamed, she screamed so loudly it felt like everybody in Faith's Creek could hear it. Her face was red, her throat hoarse from screeching. Beth tried to comfort her, wishing she would stop. It felt like she'd been crying forever. Timothy, with heavy bags under his eyes, looked to the wailing Abigail, and then to his *fraa*, silently imploring her to make the noise stop. But they both were exhausted from Abigail's woes, they didn't know what to do.

"I've tried everything," Beth admitted, at a total loss.

"What's wrong with her?" Timothy asked, he'd never seen Abigail like this.

Just when they both felt at their absolute wits' end, the door opened, and help came into the room. Crossing like an angel, taking Abigail in her arms, and finally bringing silence to the room. Beth and Timothy breathed sighs of relief.

The angel that came in was Abigail Freeman, and the screaming Abigail was Beth and Timothy's baby, named after her as a *denke* for her being there during the birth. It had been a tough six months of no sleep for the new parents, but Abigail did the best she could for them, often coming around to give them breaks.

"*Denke*," Beth said, enjoying the silence.

"She's teething is all. Rub a bit of the ointment on her gums, that will help. Now, hurry up and get dressed or you'll miss the wedding."

bigail, looking beautiful in her simple blue dress and prayer *Kapp*, was waiting outside the barn. Inside were the

inhabitants of Faith's Creek, with one exception of course. Samuel wasn't there. As Maria checked her *dochder*'s appearance, Abigail inquired, "How is *Daed* coping with the Samuel situation? Is he still kicking up a stink?"

Maria waved it away. "He can kick up what he wants. I don't know what we were thinking arranging a union with that man. He's hard-nosed and thinks himself above us, and the more I got to know him the more I think he's selfish. I'm so angry at us for ever pushing the two of you together."

"*Jah*, but still... you were only looking out for me, you were doing what seemed right, it is time to forget it now."

"My lovely, put it out of your mind. This is your day. You and Jonah. We're so happy that he's back, and that you're marrying him. And anyway, Jonah and Timothy have formed a strong bond, we can forget Samuel. So don't worry about a thing. Just enjoy this. The beginning of the rest of your married life."

With those words said, Abigail let the occasion rise up to meet her. This was an event she had begun to believe would never happen. She had tried to move on from it, but in truth, there was always a tiny corner of her heart that hoped and prayed it would come to pass... and here it was.

Abigail and Jonah exchanged their vows in front of all the people they loved. They beamed through them, they were so happy. Bishop Beiler was also smiling, he was aware of what they'd gone through to reach this point, and it made him all the more thankful to *Gott* that they'd found their righteous path. He had also been instrumental in the Elder's decision to let Jonah come back into the fold. He reminded them all what it had been like to be that young and assured them he'd seen into both of their hearts and knew this union would last.

After the ceremony, as the applause cheers, and love from the district rang out through the barn, Jonah and Abigail stole a few seconds outside. They both felt like they were walking on clouds.

"Well, hello Mrs. Harrison," Jonah smiled.

"Hello to you, too, Mr. Harrison," Abigail replied. They both felt like kids on Christmas day, standing before the present they'd been hoping for. Jonah took

Abigail in his arms, and she felt like she fit within them like a flowing river within its bed.

"I can't believe I even thought about never coming back. I was such an idiot. To think this nearly didn't happen. It could be you here, with Samuel."

"Don't... that doesn't bear thinking about."

"And me, living a very sad life, miserable in a completely different city."

Abigail shivered that the thought of such a different future for both of them. Different from the idyllic one she now faced.

"I wish I'd never even gone on my Rumspringa," Jonah confessed.

"I don't. I'm glad you did."

Jonah looked at her incredulously. How could she say that?

"I won't pretend it's not been hard. But I have grown up this past year and a half. The pain of losing you taught me how to value the life we have. Isn't that the purpose of a Rumspringa, to see something else of life? A different way. And to then decide what you want. If you hadn't gone, we would be here now, married, but we wouldn't value it as much as we do. And in time, we might have come to take it for granted. Wondering if there was a different choice we could have made. As it is our love was tested and it came through. We kept the faith and we are here, happy, fulfilled and in love still."

Jonah looked at Abigail with such pride. She was so wise and so right. He couldn't believe how lucky he was to have her as his *fraa*.

"So I'm glad you went. But I'm over the moon that you came back to me. Eventually."

She wrapped her arms around him, kissed him as his *fraa*, and then pulled him in for an all-encompassing embrace.

"I promise you," Jonah whispered into her ear, "I'll never leave you again."

"Don't worry," Abigail smiled, "I won't let you."

They kissed once more and went back into the barn, where they were greeted by her parents, Beth and Timothy, Amos and Sarah Beiler, the whole of

Faith's Creek, and the wondrous magnificence of *Gott*.

All of them looked at the newly married couple, and they all silently knew that these two would be happy for a very, very long time.

Annie Baker sat in the conservatory of the *haus* she shared with her husband, peering out at a world blanketed in snow. She was the middle of four schweschders, all of whom had always loved the spring, truly coming alive when the world around them began to wake up. Annie smiled to think of the three of them hibernating now, tucking themselves away in their separate homes and waiting for the world's warmth to return.

As for her, Annie couldn't have been more different if she had set out to be so. She was never more alive than she was when it was cold outside. She looked forward to feeling the first chill in the air all year long, and the colder it got, the more alive she felt.

As far as she remembered, and according to her *mamm's* telling of things, she had been that way for as long as she could walk on two legs. Her *mamm* was fond of telling anyone who would listen that she had practically needed to tie Annie to her skirts to keep her from running out into the snow when she was small, so enamored had she been with the idea of a winter wonderland.

Now, she was thirty-years-old, however, and as much as she would have loved to go frolicking through the flurries for as long as the daylight would allow, she had to content herself with sitting where she could see the light fall of snow and feel the chill seeping in through the windows. There was a pile of mending in a wicker basket at her feet around which Marmalade, the orange cat that had adopted the Baker *familye* as his own, was sniffing.

"What is it, Marmalade?" she asked with a low laugh, reaching down and scratching him between the ears. "Are you trying to help me with my mending? Because something tells me you might do more harm than good."

Marmalade mewed indignantly and took one last turn around her basket before prancing off to the window. He hopped up onto the sill and pressed his face against the glass, a sight that made Annie laugh all over again. The cat, always intent on looking dignified, looked exactly like a *kinner* awaiting a visitor with excitement he could hardly contain.

"All right," she sighed, laying her work aside and getting to her feet. "What is it, Marmalade? What do you see that you find so fascinating out there?"

She reached for the sweet spot between his ears again, still smiling happily as she looked out the window beside him. When she saw what her sometimes pet was watching so intently, though, something in her smile changed. If somebody were to pass by and look in at that exact moment, he would likely think her the saddest woman in the world.

Because it was a group of *kinner*. That was what

Marmalade was watching with such interest. It was a small band of *kinner* romping and playing in the snow in exactly the same way she had done when she was young.

It wasn't a longing to return to her own youth that brought the sense of acute melancholy rushing over her. She had never been the sort of woman to dwell on the years going by, instead choosing to be grateful for each new minute that *Gott* decided to gift her with.

"They're so precious, aren't they?" she whispered.

She was ostensibly talking to Marmalade but really to herself, seeing as the cat had already lost interest and had gone on his way. It made *nee* difference to her, though, not really. In actual fact, she was really talking to herself. She was talking to the only part of her that could not find peace and happiness with the life she currently lived.

Annie had known that she wanted to have *kinner* of her own since she was a little girl herself. She had always been happy to help her *mamm* caring for her younger *schweschders*, secretly pretending that they were her own. As she grew up, she began looking towards the future; she dreamed almost nightly of what her life would be like. Whether waking or sleeping, nee matter how hard she tried to keep her focus on the present, she thought of what lay ahead of her. She imagined what it would be like to find the person *Gott* intended for her and to know the joy of becoming a *fraa*. And with that vision, there was always a *haus* full of *kinner*, the sound of their joyful laughter filling the hallways as well as her heart.

She had known Mathew since she was a small girl, but it hadn't been until she was seventeen and he nineteen that she began to realize that the feelings she harbored for him were more than friendship. She had been thrilled beyond measure when he had revealed that he felt the same way, and after a short courtship, the two of them were wed.

Now, she was the *fraa* she had always seen herself being with a husband she loved. She said *denke* to *Gott* for each and every day. Her life was full of more blessings than she could count, and she knew that she should be happy. The only problem was the lingering silence in her *haus*, broken only by the occasional mewing of Marmalade. There were *nee kinner, nee boppli* to fill her arms. Though she knew it was wrong, that she must have patience, she felt a deep and terrible loneliness that would not pass.

"Hello?" a voice called from the back of the *haus*, almost as if to put an end to her sadness over the silence in her home. "Where are you, my love?"

"I'm in the conservatory!" she called, smiling despite the melancholy seeing the *kinner* had brought on. "Marmalade and I were trying to work on the mending, but I'm afraid we didn't get as far as I would have hoped."

Despite her dark thoughts, Annie's heart soared as she heard her husband's heavy, boot-clad footsteps approach. She still felt this same kind of excitement every time she heard him come home, even after just over twelve years of marriage. He was not only the love of her life, but he was also her best friend, something she was thankful for beyond measure.

"Well, here you are!" he exclaimed, stepping into the doorway and smiling at her lovingly. "Your helper wandered down the hall past me just a moment ago, so not so helpful after all, is he? Maybe it's time we get rid of him."

"*Nee!*" Annie said with a laugh, opening her arms to

embrace Mathew, who still wore a coat with snow-dusted shoulders. "I've told you, we can't ever let Marmalade go. He wouldn't stand for it. And besides, he may be the closest thing to a *kinner* I ever have."

"*Ach,* my dear," Mathew sighed, kissing her on the tip of her nose and pulling back some so he could get a look at her. "Why do you say such things? Are you having one of your bad days?"

Annie shrugged and wrapped her arms around herself, holding herself tightly and hating the fact that she had enough hard days for her husband to be able to comment on them thus. She would have liked to tell him that he was wrong, but the sound of the *kinner's* laughter came again from outside, and he nodded to himself as if to show that he understood.

"It's nothing," Annie said, swallowing down her sorrow and putting on a sweet smile, if only for Mathew's benefit. "I just got a little bit lost in my own head, that's all. There's nothing for you to worry about, especially because you must be starving after a long day of work!"

She tried to slip past him, wanting to keep him from

seeing the pain still in her eyes. He took her gently by the shoulders, though, stopping her in her tracks and looking down at her with such intensity that she had *nee* choice but to return his gaze. His eyes were a deep, vibrant green and were full of such intensity of purpose at the moment that it nearly took her breath away.

"Please, Annie," he murmured softly, raising one hand to caress her cheek gently. "Please, don't do this to yourself. There's *nee* reason to think that hope is lost."

"Isn't there?" she laughed, although there was little humor in the sound. "It's been twelve years, Mathew. If we were going to have a *boppli,* don't you think we would have done so by now?"

"*Nee,*" he said earnestly, tugging at his reddish-blonde beard thoughtfully. "Honestly, I don't. It's not for us to decide when these things happen. *Gott* might choose to bless us with a *boppli* whenever He sees fit. It's not for us to choose nor to question."

"I know, Mathew," she said, barely able to speak above a whisper now. "And I try to remember that, but in my heart of hearts, I know that I will never have a *kinner*. It's me, that's the problem. It's my fault. Something is wrong with me."

And with that, Annie began to cry. It was a conversation the two of them had had more times than she could count over the years. It was as painful now as if they were having it for the very first time. She had *nee* idea how many more times they would have in the future before she was finally able to find peace with her lot in life. All she knew for sure was that she believed what she was telling Mathew with her whole heart. She would never deliver a *boppli*, *nee* matter how much she wanted to. She could feel in her bones that it was not a privilege meant for her to have, and despite all of her other good fortune, it all but broke her heart.

Grab the Amish Spring Baby Box Set for FREE with Kindle unlimited

AMISH ROMANCE
Amish
SPRING BABY
4 BOOK BOX SET
SARAH MILLER
BABY DILEMMA
BABY SURPRISE
BABY BLESSING
BABY JOY

Find all Sarah's books on Amazon and click the yellow follow button

This book is dedicated to the wonderful Amish people and the faithful life that they live.

Go in peace my friends.

As an independent author, Sarah relies on your support. If you enjoyed this book, please leave a review on Amazon or Goodreads.

ABOUT THE AUTHOR

Sarah Miller was born in Pennsylvania and spent her childhood close to the Amish people. Weekends were spent doing chores; quilting or eventually babysitting in the community. She grew up to love their culture and the simple lifestyle and had many Amish friends. The one thing that you can guarantee when you are near the Amish, Sarah believes is that you will feel close to God.

Many years later she married Martin who is the love of her life and moved to England. There she started to write stories about the Amish. Recently after a lot of persuasion from her best friend she has decided to publish her stories. They draw on inspiration from her relationship with the Amish and with God and she hopes you enjoy reading them as much as she did writing them. Many of the stories are based on true events but names have been changed and even though they are authentic at times artistic license has been used.

Sarah likes her stories simple and to hold a message and they help bring her closer to her faith. She currently lives in Yorkshire, England with her husband Martin and seven very spoiled chickens.

She would love to meet you on Facebook at https://www.facebook.com/SarahMillerBooks

Sarah hopes her stories will both entertain and inspire and she wishes that you go with God.